OTHER WILD

ALSO BY EMILY ZOBEL MARSHALL

POETRY
Bath of Herbs (2023)

NONFICTION
Anansi's Journey: A Story of Jamaican Cultural Resistance (2012)
American Trickster: Trauma Tradition and Brer Rabbit (2019).

EDITED
Oluwale Now: An Anthology of Poetry, Prose and Artwork Responding to the Story of David Oluwale (2023, ed. with Sai Murray).

TO THEO AND ROSE

EMILY ZOBEL MARSHALL

OTHER WILD

PEEPAL TREE

First published in Great Britain in 2025
Peepal Tree Press Ltd
17 King's Avenue
Leeds LS6 1QS
UK

ISBN 13: 9781845236045

Cover art: "Other Wild" by Kezia Lewis

EU GPSR Authorised Representative
LOGOS EUROPE,
9 rue Nicolas Poussin,
17000, LA ROCHELLE, France

Supported using public funding by
ARTS COUNCIL
ENGLAND

CONTENTS

Section I: Everywhere River

How to Get Back into Your Body 11
How you Rose 12
Poem for Rose 13
Lemons, Tomorrow 14
Otter 15
Come, Mami Wata 16
Goldfinch 17
You Come to Me in Birds 18
Through Road 19
Siesta 20
Us 21
Chernobyl Birthday 22
Only the Bracken Remembers 23
On My Side 24
Rock Cakes 25
When I Return 26
Sky Claim 28
The Dive 29
Son, Paused 30
There Are Days 31
Night Rain 32
Sky Light 33
Somewhere Between Us 34
Looking for Answers in the Fog 35
In Hope of Lightness 36
The Island 37
A Prayer for Light in Lisbon 39
Pause 40
Petrichor 41
Chesil Beach 42
Grading Benches 43
To Gather Moss 44

Waterfall Scramble   45
Toad   46
Small Boats   47
White Egrets   48
Song of the Archive   49

II: The Shape of Trees

Blind Night   53
Block   54
House Martins   55
Wooden Boulder   56
Dreaming Trees   57
The Shape of Trees   58
Frost Flowers   59
Ashes to Ashes   60
Synoptic Forecasts   61
Now, She Plants   62
All My Lovin'   63
Why I Hated You at the Bus Shelter   64
No Point Crying over Spilt Milk   66
I Live Here   67
Mami's Visit   68
J'étais Belle   69
On Staying Close   70
Birthday Card   71
Disappearing Dad   72
Für Elise   73
Things We Might Have Done on Your Birthday   74
Smaller Things   76
The Autumn Wind Blows Through the Sycamores   77
Retreat   78

III: Other Wild

Left   81
The Ptarmigan   82
Tall Tale   83
Breeze   84
Elsewhere   85
Hide and Seek   86
Nurse Charlotte   87
Cartwheeling   88
Oluwale Rising   90
Witch   92
You Show Me Yours and I'll Show You Mine   93
Lane Share   94
Dick Pic   95
To the Range Rover Asshole   96
Conduit   97
To Smell Like Sky   98
Mardi Gras Under the Freeway   99
I Need Milk Too   100
Martinique, I Hear   102
Blodeuwedd   103
What To Call Me?   104
Women are Only Free   105
You Tell Me a Desire Line   106
When I Emptied My Moon Cup on the Mountain   107
Let Me Map You, He Said   108

Acknowledgements   109

I: EVERYWHERE RIVER

HOW TO GET BACK INTO YOUR BODY

Sometimes, when you need to return
to your body, a frozen river can help.

The burning cold can cauterise the wounds
etched on your flimsy heart, call the body back.

Break thin ice and wade. The river-pull will
tug flesh and bone, unknot ankles, grasp

the curve of your hips, pinch your nipples,
clutch your ribcage so tight

you are lung-squeezed to take a breath
so deep your wandering body returns.

Listen. You can hear your new sub-aquatic
blood-coursing rhythms. They sound like hope. Like rivers.

HOW YOU ROSE
For Rose

When you swim
you send snakes of Spring sunlight
slithering across dark waters
from bank to bank.

Entranced by your circling stroke,
I wonder at how you rose cleanly
from the suck of treacherous currents
over and over again.

While Dad and I knew all the timings,
memorised the names of drugs,
it was you who learnt
to move your body forwards.

I see the tight muscles in your back,
the surprise of slick long hair;
your healing was determined
by your own stroke.

I slide into the river, tail you
as you move through dappled rays,
your strong bare feet kicking
great kaleidoscopic arcs of spray, skywards.

POEM FOR ROSE

If I was tempted to write the same poem
over and over again, it would be one
which maps your body, the way
your little toe bends inwards
(a baby slug curled into a lettuce leaf)
or details how every hair on your head
surprises in its swinging straightness,
how I am stilled watching the tiny flare
of your sleeping nostrils or tracing
the galaxy of summer freckles
settled on your nose.

But when I hold the sweeping slope
of your brown back in the crook of my arm
and see distant clouds reflected in your eyes,
I think, perhaps, you are my poem
and I should rest my pen.

LEMONS, TOMORROW

Early December,
I walked a muddied footpath
along the River Wharfe
to forget your diagnosis,
and I remembered the lemon trees
on that Greek island after the rain –
citrine gems throwing fresh
antiseptic scents into sapphire skies,
mingling with the tang of goat dung,
fruit winter-ripened, storing last summer's heat,
crystal droplets clinging to sunset rinds,
their perfume on the breeze long after
the clear disk of the Spring moon
has pierced the ocean's skin.

So I brought you lemons,
grated and squeezed, added amber honey,
a steaming bedside brew in an NHS mug.
You wouldn't drink much, but through
nose and throat I hoped you'd travel
to a small Ionian island, ripe lemons after the rain,
a clean smell of hope, not hospitals.

OTTER

Arms encircle dark waters –
suddenly she is there,
fresh pelt glistening,
mouth all teeth and bite.

She swims dog-like,
head above water, fish-like below;
my body next to hers
clumsy in brown flesh.

She leaves, bank slithering
unhurried, body looping
like a shining alphabet S.

Nothing left behind,
only cotton clouds drifting
across a mirroring river,
its ripples steadying.

COME, MAMI WATA

Come, Mami Wata, charmer of serpents,
calmer with water-cool hands,
siren signaller of sailor-death,
Middle Passage guardian,
womb-space warden,
healer of diasporic agony,
I see you man-strung, tired,
dragged to the surface of boiling seas.

Come, you are safe in the slipstream
of this girl-river-swimmer, daughter
of land, at home in Yorkshire waters.
Come, many-faced African womanfish,
push upriver from grey Northern seas;
with migrating salmon energy, you'll find me.

I'll adorn your riverbank bower
with marsh marigolds, waxy silver lilies.
My son will fish you minnow suppers.
I'll show you where otters play;
you can stroke their shining, muscled pelts.

Crowned with cow-parsley,
come rest in my pool,
lying on your back, river currents
tickling your knotted spine like a lover,
watching a mango-ripe sun
pour golden over the Wharfe.

GOLDFINCH

In your final days, when you're in the mood for chat,
you tell me that you're so content you could embrace yourself;

you've seen the world and watched your grandkids grow,
your kids will be okay without you, that you know.

We've wheeled your hospice bed outside to catch the sun;
the fountain sparkles in its rays; in the oak a goldfinch chirps.

Nurse brings you a lolly; I prop your head and help you slurp
and think that even if it's just the morphine kicking in,

there's little more to wish for, in our final days of travelling,
than to feel contentment and to want to hug ourselves,
as we listen to a goldfinch sing.

YOU COME TO ME IN BIRDS

When I see no line of flight between the clouds,
and all my dreams are long deferred,
you come to me in birds.

When my day is slate-slab grey and shadows prey,
when all is dark and I am bruised
with aching for your touch,
you send a wren.

It lands so close it must be there to speak,
trembling beneath the broadening leaves
of beech, and so I rise to greet this song
from your beyond.

Perhaps a mirage of the mourning heart,
but with every bird you bring I hear
the messages they sing.
I'm listening.

THROUGH-ROAD

This dream was about a through-road,
not a shortcut,
insisted my dream-narrator,
but a through-road.

In the moment when my body
was hollowed from aching
for your touch, and my ears
strained to catch the song of your voice,
I took a through-road
from anywhere, from elsewhere,
travelling sure as a summer swift
back to you.

SIESTA

The forest relents and wilts,
baking earth sleeps,
only the cicadas chirp
into syrupy air
as heat-drugged fat black ants
zig-zag their way
up the whitewashed bedroom wall

In the shuttered house
time for the infernal *siesta,*
my family spread-eagled on tangled beds,
limbs twisted in damp sheets
willing the whirring fans
to cool their fevered hours.

I long for escape
from Mami's thick-walled cloisters,
railing against the afternoon nap
and enforced sleep,
dreaming of sweet release
in the cool currents of the Gardon river,
of the soft-mouthed feel
of minnows nibbling ankles,
of sinking down to the riverbed, of lying
looking up through the blurring flow
to the relentless sun
blazing in the blue,
knowing it can't find me
and burn my cool, suspended limbs

I float like this in visions
until evening and the promise of
cooler air begins to whisper
across the Cevennol sky.

us

When it's morning, we don't know
where our limbs begin and end –
skin is the only thing between *you* and *me*
and I wonder how the years have kept us
so entwined, even when we swim away,
pushing towards the farthest shore,
our circles widening in the blue,
but we arc back in and tangle
limbs once more, drawn by the scent
of *us* on early morning skin.

CHERNOBYL BIRTHDAY

Eighth birthday. Nearly everyone from the village is in the field outside our house. The farmer brings 80-year-old Nelly in his Land Rover. Not fair for her to miss the fun. Big deal as we can't normally get a car down the mile-long track to Garth-y-Foel.

Warm for late April. Perfect picnic weather, though the peaks of the Moelwyns and Cnicht still holding fast a dusting of snow. We are in our pants. All the kids from school turn up. Squish of mud between bare toes. Leap-frogging.

Mum brings out my cake – gooey chocolate, baked in four loaf-tins with red icing and covered in multi-coloured smarties. A triumph. Robin-the-neighbour organises rounders. Even Nelly joins in. The horse trots into the field, tossing his mane, much admired. The Mums spread winter-white legs out on picnic blankets. Dads crack open beers.

The rain starts suddenly. Out of nowhere. Heavy but not cold. April showers. Adults hurry armfuls of blankets inside. We stay out, skidding on wet grass, drenched through. until Mum shouts: *Inside, now! You'll catch your death out there.*

School drop-off the next day. The parents huddle in the playground. Nuclear disaster. Alerted the Trawsfynydd power station, but not the locals. Radioactivity in the rain. Kids out in it. I think about the leftover cake in my lunch box. I've counted the smarties. Sixteen – one for each kid in school. Still living. The best birthday ever...

ONLY THE BRACKEN REMEMBERS

how you felt, photographed
naked in that Welsh waterfall.

The picture speaks to me of freedom.
I'm envious of this woman caught
before all the difficult things, of you
in black and white, grinning
in July sunlight, river dividing itself
around your smooth, dark,
sundering body.

You let this friend from the village
snap you in this secret place,
jade bracken-carpeted valley,
let him catch you in the late afternoon,
Afro haloed in silver light,
strewn with gossamer droplets,
nipples high, pointed with cold,
lashes webbed in water mist,
cascade rush fixed by a hungry lens.

Are you urging Dad towards jealousy?
Thinking you can't back out?
Camera-hidden, is your friend
distilling a moment of beauty?
Will he return to this photo
alone in his dark room, again and again?

In the tugging silence of time,
there's only my story to whisper into yours.
I choose to see freedom,
but only the bracken remembers.

ON MY SIDE

I walk onto the bus and into pain,
each taunt a rock thrown with precision.
Because I walk in wellies, I'm a *sheep-shagger;*
because my nose is wide, I'm *nostrils;*
my big and curly 'fro makes me *bushchild.*

Outside the bus window,
sun dances through the Spring leaves,
bathing my white shirt, my striped tie,
and I look up at the aquamarine sky,
imagine myself small, a fleck
in an ever-shifting solar system –
and what happens on the school bus
is nothing – passing wind-blown dust.

I see that my cwm is embraced
by the mountains that know me,
and by the ice-clear Croesor river;
and the starry mosses balancing dewdrops
in morning light, the towering
head-nodding bracken, and the horse,
steaming in his paddock, are on my side.

ROCK CAKES

I had baked you rock cakes
cooling now on the Welsh dresser;
I'd planned all our chat,
the things I'd show you: garden, horse,
play my best Bob Marley tape. I'm all
cherry-red lipstick, mum's perfume,
Afro in coconut-oil-shine –
even brought a cloth to wipe my
Doc Martens clean from cowshit – all planned
so that when you saw me from the bus
in my Glastonbury tassel skirt,
it would be love.

Every hour I go to meet the bus,
dodge the cowpats there and back.
Cakes cold now, Mum's eyes full of a feeling
I wish she'd keep to herself.
Dusk falls; the cakes go to my brother,
who shares one with the dog. I prepare
my uniform for the next day, adrift.

As I walk into school, I hear you in the cloakroom,
loud towny-boy laugh: *As if I'd*
visit her in the sticks. I feel a surge
from somewhere belly-deep: *You've been dumped.*
Shouted in front of everyone. And there's a thick silence
because it wasn't for someone like me
to finish with a boy like you,
and I'm gulping back a lump
the size of a rock cake,
hoping it won't delay
the thickening of new skin.

WHEN I RETURN

When I return to my childhood home, I remember
there were poisons on the doorstep, towering spears

of monkshood deadly enough, Mum said, to kill a lamb,
or small child, its loveliness deceptive;

and when you pee by the laburnum, don't hold its trunk –
it will burn, blister, welt a child's skin; and there are hauntings

everywhere of suffering ghosts – Mabinogion Elen
who, on hearing of her son's death impaled by an arrow,

wept tears that formed a spring, crying *Croes awr i mi*, 'This
is my cursed hour' – which our mountain village was named

after; and as for the neighbouring farmhouse, Parc,
its insides are so rafter-packed with ghosts that they jostle for room,

spilling out into the yard already filled with the spirits of Cromwell's
men thirsty for the blood of monks; and in the gloaming, the air

becomes thick with the clatter of horses until they evaporate
into night; and there's the memories of blood, my head cracked

like an egg on the slate floor after a karate chop by my brother;
and there's this window right here which his head smashed

after I grabbed his legs as he sat on the sill of my bedroom –
which was where Mrs Lloyd Williams died of shock

a hundred years ago after getting her skirts caught in a butter churn,
or so they said (we could hear her wailing still).

When I head back to Leeds along the snaking green tunnel
of the Croesor road, I beg every electrifying Welsh story

and spirit to follow me home to soulless suburbia,
and teach me how to live again.

SKY CLAIM

Does Mum see me
as I cut a line
between earth and sky,
across heather and peat bog,
along zig-zagging sheep tracks
in a bright red anorak?

These fells have rarely seen
mixedness like mine,
but I walk boldly
over ragged ridges
clawed by dying bracken,
knowing that in Spring
the hosts of golden daffodils
belong to me.

As the crescent moon rises
like an unfinished question,
I marry map to compass
and feel her hand
gentle on my back,
urging me to climb and claim
this earth and rock,
this moon and sky.

THE DIVE

We watch you teetering on the edge of the three-meter board
and forget to breathe. Awakened from echoing, stifling, municipal pool

chlorine semi-slumber, we are fixed on your 8-year-old body,
poised high above water. We feel each plasticky bend and warp as

you bounce, testing for the perfect velocity to launch
yourself, and then flight – winter sunlight hitting your

little torso, Lego man pushed off a cliff, tiny brown pebble
thrown into a lake. Double back-somersault, tucked rose-bud-tight

to uncurl just before impact, a silent glide, leaving only
rippling circles, a sea bird diving for fish, swooping

from blue sky to a waiting ocean, and as you emerge laughing,
shaking your curls like a wet dog, we breathe again,

knowing we should always trust the bond between you
and the water, which welcomes your body so.

SON, PAUSED

Son, I love to watch you fish,
your coiled curls catching the sun,
only you, rod poised,
river, reel and line
and the innocent bob
of the lure.

Son, dreaming always
of dappled trout,
of the promise beneath,
your current of wild
13-year-old energy
stilled.

Son, curls, silver line ready,
river running,
son,
paused.

THERE ARE DAYS
For Theo

There are days, tension-knotted,
when you rail against me:
I won't buy you steak for dinner,
won't give you iPhone time for games,
won't stop talking too loudly.
You wish me smaller, more compliant,
less unbending, less proud
less forthright, less…

And there are days,
easy in my company,
when you let your hand slip into mine
leave it there while you tell me
in a rare moment of chattiness
about your plans beyond the now,
and together we see them hang there
in all their future fullness.
Let us remember these days.

NIGHT RAIN

In the wide-awake hour before midnight,
after summer-thickened days,
night rain drumming on the thirsty earth,
we leave our windows open to the night,
watch trees luminesce as leaves bow to water
finding its way through every fissure,
letting folds of memory unfurl.

On nights like these we slide
into newly opened crevices
to breach the space between us,
seeking out our softest parts
to reach and there remain.

SKY LIGHT

Lately, I have noticed
the blurring of you and I
happening in the new room
in the attic of the old house,
where the rain pulses hard on the pane.

No clear moment marking it – perhaps
watching all those open-window
midnights and sunrises together
latticed a bandage tough enough
to hold back breaking,
fine enough to let the sky in.

SOMEWHERE BETWEEN US AND THE TOWERING UMBELLIFERS

we feel a widening, an expansion outwards
which only happens at midsummer when evening
comes and bats dart the sky. We feel as if we can see
the trees grow if we stand still enough, and the
lines and edges between us and the clouds of cow parsley
become blurred, our skin its skin, our beating hearts the rush
of the brook, the bleat of sheep, our blood the sap swelling
through the sycamore, pushing up through our shoes
and filling us whole.

LOOKING FOR ANSWERS IN THE FOG

The sea must be there. I hear her muffled waves crash and heave, her salty gasp below me, summersaulting smoothed pebbles. I stare into the beyond; no horizons reveal themselves. I thought that to stand at the brink of something vast would help make sense of things. I'd hoped for remedies in cliffs, in surf and swell, in breath grabbed by the wind, in rain-jewelled eyelashes. But I stand blind at the land's edge. I return home, head bent against then wind. Walking. My only comfort being its heart-beat, foot-beat rhythm.

IN HOPE OF LIGHTNESS

Should you walk down to the shore
below the cliffs, you'll hear the seals
gently croon and coo as they lie
on hot rocks like soft, scattered stones,
helpless bags of blubber hefting
from side-to-side to stay cool while
the tide gently rises and waves start to
lick fat mottled stomachs until
temptation overcomes and they slip
into the water, transformed now,
streamlined, diving deep and slick,
glistening heads surfacing,
sighing sea breath, weightless
now and ocean-wed.

Let me be a seal in water,
not heaving my clumsy flailing loss
across sharp rocks.
Push me in.
Let's see if I glide light.

THE ISLAND

Here are the goats
descending the ridgeline,
their bells playing
a symphony of battered brass,
their wild tang marrying
the clean scents of tall cypresses,
whose branches reach towards
a sapphire sky.

In the olive grove,
the unharvested trees' creased
frowning trunks crouch
against ocean winds,
their snaking roots
gripping hard
the shallow terraces.

Jerusalem sage spreads
beneath clinging juniper bushes,
and fine tendrils of vetch
embrace with bees,
sacks fat with pollen,
humming across tangles of rock roses,
dipping deep into the secret purses
of maiden's tears.

Love-in-the mist
quietly rubs our thighs
in the tiny graveyard,
where the long-dead stare
from creased photos
in salt-tarnished golden frames,
on white tombs facing the waves.

Observe goats, groves, wildflowers,
honeybees, ruins, cemetery
and restless ocean.
Walk into the lazuline sea,
let it suck, let it lap your skin
as it turns and turns,
for only this, only this exists.

A PRAYER FOR LIGHT IN LISBON

River Tagus, I walk in the city's shadows
but you make me dream of light. I came to mourn,
but you keep me spell-struck in this city
that scatters glitter across my battered boots,
that throws sunlight onto rusty tiled roofs
and under the wings of circling gulls,
setting bougainvillea and hibiscus tumbling
ablaze from balconies, blinding the eye with silver fire,
so even fisherman forget to fish, and dream only
of the snakes of mercury streaking your silver skin.

River Tagus, I'll lie weightless in your arms
as you cast me out under the bridge, into the span
of your ocean, so that deep in your midnight trenches
I can whisper my secrets of darkness,
and return baptised, hearing only silence
between the dip of oars, being filled with the light
shuddering across your waves, and being hurled up
over your banks, strewn across the city to shine,
unburdened and alive with your flow swaying in my hips,
smiling from your miracle dewed on my lips.

PAUSE

Lately, the days are pressed thin.
No birdsong, no plump sun rising,
morning light banished from the sky,
the day halted before its birth,
and underfoot, a film of dirt
coating roads, mud-sucking feet.

Clawed by these midwinter endings,
looking to understand the pause,
I find a swell begun on buds of birch,
catch a yellow shock of bloom on gorse.
I listen to the wind raking
through an old stone wall,
trying to sense the gathering within,
to hear it speak of Spring.

PETRICHOR

The day has barely risen from its pillow
yet my plane has flown across time zones
on this endless red-eye flight
away from you.

Glued to my tiny window,
I see celestial painters brush the sky
with palettes of burning pink,
scoop cirrus in swirls of apricot
as earth shows off her endless curves
to the rising sun.

I remember how you once
told me the exact name
for the welcome scent of rain
on long-dry earth –
from Greek 'petra', meaning stone,
and 'ichor', the golden fluid
pumping through the veins
of immortals.

Now in flight, I know
I will stay parched,
my chest a stone, fossilized
from wanting your wetness –
my petrichor.

CHESIL BEACH

On this pebbled shore, beside
a churning winter ocean, you tell me stories,
and your hands dance to the music of your words.

I long to reach across the picnic blanket
and warm your long fingers,
fold your soft palms in mine.

But I will wait until your dance is over
for while it's not for words of love you reach,
I read the language of your hands

and understand their speech.
They tell me to stay still and by your side
on this endless stretch of beach.

GRADING BENCHES

Dad, going off on one –
stories pool and eddy, tributaries of tales
joining a main flow,
but often meandering,
branching into many smaller,
unexpected streams
so lengthy we all forget their
source and destination.

This time, though, it's not reflections
on 'the youth' or recounting close
encounters with a menagerie of wild animals,
no insistence on your radicalism,
weighty penmanship or physical prowess
(not bad, eh, for nearly 80?), but
an anecdote on a pastime new to me:
grading benches.

How, across the Med, alongside Nana,
you strolled and sat and graded:
points for comfort, design,
placement and the view.
This story doesn't multiply itself
but brings a softness to your face.
Perhaps, I think, one day I'll also rest a while,
take my time to grade a bench or two.

TO GATHER MOSS

You're always *on the move*, says Granny.
Well, a rolling stone gathers no moss, I reply.
Sad for the stone, she says; I love moss.
You've misunderstood the saying, I begin to explain,
and then I see this moss, soft and fecund, forest
lifeblood, supporting eco systems of grandchildren,
mycelium networks of aging friends and villagers.
The stone that rolls alone is all hard edges, no roots.
If my rock slowed a little, let the moss grow, it could
sit damp and dappled on the woodland floor
sustaining life across its hard, unyielding back.

WATERFALL SCRAMBLE

We squeeze into impossible shapes,
climb a rockfall split and streaked red
with earth's old blood,
trace water's ghosts
high up jagged, slimy crevasses.

Rain begins to fall sideways,
eye-blurring, with a deep-bone reach,
dislodging feet from shallow ledges
as the river starts to rush.

Now all is survival, is urge to live.
We pause in silent prayer
to mountain's rock and water:
Let us pass unharmed up your great artery
and forgive give us for our trespasses.
We know we don't belong.

TOAD

Spring is urgent in woodland:
sky-bound shoots push through
leafmould, yet in the muddied pond
the coupling toads hang silent.

When shouting children drag them
from the water's edge, they return,
clinging together, a clod of forest floor
making slow, ungainly headway home.

Threats of hunting herons
do not release his slender fingers,
nor break his endless clutch
across her broad flat back.

This quiet embrace
of stippled prehistoric skin
pulses stronger than
the fear of endings.

SMALL BOATS

The 'clock is ticking' to stop small boat crossings in the Channel (Priti Patel, May 2023)

'*We will pass new laws to stop small boats, making sure that if you come to this country illegally, you are detained and swiftly removed*' (Rishi Sunak, Jan 2023)

'*Without tougher controls on immigration… we risk becoming an island of strangers, not a nation that walks forward together.*' (Keir Starmer, May 2025)

On my small boat the waves
seem to pause and listen, then carry on throwing us about.
In the pauses, I try and understand
why Mum brought me here.

She doesn't want to look at me;
says there are too many of us all squashed together.
Though she holds me, we are still cold.
The night presses on my eyelids,
fills me with salt-breath.

I used to swim with my best friend.
Then, the sea was calm and kind,
kept me floating, eyes half-closed in the sun's rays.
This sea's wild,
wants to finish off this small boat.

I want to reach where the clouds lift,
where we can see our tomorrow.
I want to see daybreak
and me and Mum still floating, suspended
on smooth, mirroring, silken water.

WHITE EGRETS

Beneath a mottled sky,
white egrets wait to peck silver fish
on this placid California seashore.
I am, for once, in no hurry,
so I stay a while, struck by their skeletal grace,
and make promises to sit with this stillness
before striking out again, to let all action flow
from calmer seas.

SONG OF THE ARCHIVE

Between 1500 and 1866 an estimated 1.8 million enslaved Africans died during the Middle Passage of the Transatlantic slave trade. Their bodies were thrown overboard.

Walcott and Nichols tell us our archive lies
beneath the water, that between us
and your story is the barrier of the Middle Passage,
a song-muting, fact-crushing graveyard, trying
to prevent the birth of our stories just as salt
tried to dissolve umbilical cords beneath the water.

Forebear, no official map traced your journey.
I cannot peer into the retina of your consciousness;
your eye sockets, hollowed, seep silence. Beneath
the water, your verses hide like hermit crabs,
words disappearing inside their shells when I move towards them.

I yearn to excavate your bones from the suck of tides,
from the knots of kelp forests, put my ear to your skin-stripped jaw
and hear the roar of your history from your tongue.

It cannot be done?

Perhaps, if Brer Imagination and Brer Patience help me,
keep my head bent, daylong in the archive, reading
and retracing threads with my pencil, with my keypad,
like nets drawing your stories out of water,
resurfaced, your lung-song could push up
through your dry throat, sing syllables across oceans,
touching the surface of every continent,
gliding up onto beaches, swaying across coconut trees,
paragraphs blazing through neon resorts,
your history revealing itself in its own tongue.

So while you, forebear, will never breathe again,
may your children find new spaces in their lungs
to fill with breath to sing your new-old song.
Let ears ring with it, libraries shake with it,
universities tremor with it, as we bellow
this story of your lives before the water.

II: THE SHAPE OF TREES

BLIND NIGHT

I am haunted by my dreams of you,
fearing I'll forget the timbre of your voice,
so, I climb the ridge and watch the moon
rise above the valley to ease this night-time longing.

No comfort in the rocks, no blessing
carried in the bell-heather's rattle. The gorse,
once crowned yellow, squats dark and ugly.
The leaves of silver birch watch nightwinds play
with swaying, blinking eyes. They will not look at me.

In poems, then, I'll try to write this thirst for you,
unquenched by moon, by rock and tree,
by blind, indifferent night.

BLOCK

A famous Caribbean poet said that a poet's job
is to reveal people's thoughts and feelings
to themselves, like an opening bloom.

How to do this when storms break me?

The squirrels outside my office window
don't look up. They are industrious,
finding last year's beech nuts in secret places.

How I envy them
for I cannot remember
where I buried my tongue.

HOUSE MARTINS

The house martins are nesting in the eaves;
their brood was late; now they fly silhouetted
against September sunshine, darting against a cobalt sky
to snap flies for ever-hungry chicks snuggled,
open-mouthed, in hanging nests.

See how they soar with such purpose
while I have no forwards movement,
left with pieces that don't fit back together.
I try and think them whole, but only
this emptiness exists, this inertia.

Why can't I catch syllables like flies,
bring them back to my empty pages,
fatten them with fine and juicy words?

I have been constrained from dreaming,
must fly in the slipstream of my missing presence,
must fill the holes, stuff them with little balls
of hopeful mud, repair my damaged nest
and dam this leaking heart with poems.
My first will be about house martins.
They are nesting in the eaves; their brood is late.

WOODEN BOULDER[1]

For David Nash

Wooden boulder, cast in a churning river
in a Welsh midwinter, a jagged heft
of chain-sawed oak, for 35 years tracked,
and then, errant son, hewing the water, unmapped,
did you, cleaved and chipped by winter storms,
weed-entangled, current borne,
glide past Ffestiniog slag heaps, slide out
of estuary to ocean, riding high on wave and tides?

Errant son, wooden boulder, escaping
fretful father-sculptor, fugitive from your creator,
where are you, freedom-seeker?

---

1. For 35 years the artist David Nash tracked the progress of his
sculpture, *Wooden Boulder*, described as a 'free-range sculpture', as it
travelled down the River Dwyryd in North Wales. But in 2015 the
oak sphere vanished – and Nash has been looking for it ever since.

DREAMING TREES

In a room pierced by neon streetlights,
in a night-time dream I walk beneath
thick branches holding skies alive with stars.
I dig up their twisted roots, and powered
by the moon, with dream's great strength,
drag them to my garden.

Waking, my tiny patch of city lawn
is dense with towering oaks.
Squirrels flash across their swaying tops;
birdsong drowns persistent traffic drone.
Under their canopy I drink my morning cup of tea.

THE SHAPE OF TREES

Let me climb the crag,
see the land open wide, hear the hum
of distant motorcycles, caws
of worm-hunting gulls far from sandy shores,
and sense memories of interrupted lava flow.

There, on rocks, I try to knot words
to landscape, bring images
of the blackened fingers of winter beeches
and the open palms of emerald fields.

But the distant shape of trees resists description;
each twig belongs only to itself.
I cannot name the fleeting dance of light
beneath the clouds, the final flame
of amber leaves crowning the sycamores.

Not in words, then, but rhythm –
the rise and swell of breath,
the thud of footsteps hitting frosted mud,
only in this syncopated heartbeat lies the
thing that ties me to the shape of trees.

FROST FLOWERS

Between the house and office,
the weekly shop, the children's needs,
I stand trying to remember
how to stop and watch
the frost flowers bloom,
see black crows making shadows
against frozen fields
as beams of beaten gold thrust
through the bones of trees,
spot droplets of blood hanging
in the holly tree, pierced
by its own fine prickles.

ASHES TO ASHES

We huddle in the summit shelter,
waterproofs flapping, mood low,
willing the crescent of wet, worn rock to
protect our soggy sandwiches and reddened
faces from a slicing summit wind.

It's been hellish, the kids decide,
this Boxing Day walk; dragged up a fell
from the warmth of the big blue Aga,
the womb of Granny's kitchen
for the obscure benefits of 'fresh air'.

In the midst of the arguments, the
not-sharing-of-crisps, the *I hate peanut
butter* bad behaviour, we notice the ashes
piled on a slab of greasy stone.

Stilled, the children search to understand.
A picnic beside human remains? The small
fresh-looking heap, grey powder trailing over the wall.
Did promises of casting into the wind backfire?

Was this a favourite spot, peering
into churning mists, back against cold rock?
We eat slowly now, feel the weight of endings
or flawed ritual. Not soaring freely on wild winds

over dragon-backed buttresses and ice-cleft
summits, launched closer to the stars, this
soul shelters with us here on the earth,
slowly mixing with our boot-thickened mud
and the scattered shells of hard-boiled eggs.

SYNOPTIC FORECASTS

I:

I have fallen into a deep trough,
convinced of your advancing cold front –
an icy, uncaring mass blocking all high pressure.

Occasionally, though, dense depressions
catch up with warm fronts –
we call these *occlusions*.

Balmy air rises, becoming a narrow
but burgeoning wedge,
forcing arctic atmospheres far out to sea,
signalling a return to heat, forecasting
a wrapping round of arms and legs,
of your hair spread out across my pillow.

II:

This cup of tea is
                    for the shouting

the biscuits for the
                    protracted filthy mood

embraces will come
                    but let the dark clouds lift

let the mists clear
            then, perhaps,
                        the chance of kisses...

NOW, SHE PLANTS

You didn't do planting
until after the divorce.

First came a leggy spider plant,
then its little sisters, brothers, cousins,
carefully rooted in dark compost,
small plastic pots cramped on a warm
windowsill spilling green light
across your tidy flat.

Then came flowers: a blousy pink
birthday orchid, a Christmas-gifted
supermarket poinsettia, a bird of paradise,
attentive hands keeping them blooming
longer than expected.

Emboldened, you ventured outside,
planting fragrant honeysuckle, plush ferns,
spiring ginger lilies, tall bamboo, and oily fatsias,
eucalyptus, windmill palms and cordyline.

Dad was in charge of our garden.
So proud of his stub carrots, slug-chewed
Brussels, praised as he passed them to you
for scrubbing, peeling, cooking.

But now, rooted in your suburban tropical queendom,
you plant, you grow.

ALL MY LOVIN'

All my lovin'... pipes through the car radio, flooding me
with an image of you both. You're 1970s young and you're dancing,
Dad in his flared brown cords, biting his tongue
because he's so focused on staying groovy and coordinated,
Mum flowing in a denim mini skirt,
strapless canary-yellow top, afro fluffed out
and patent white boots hugging young-girl bandy legs.

He's never met anyone like her,
this dazzling Caribbean woman, BBC job, with it *all going on*
and he, she thinks, is enthralling – maybe a little on
the small side, but with kissable full lips and a head packed
with grand ideas, ideas that will take them everywhere
when meshed with her dreams.

Close your eyes and I'll kiss you
Tomorrow I'll miss you...
they move their hips in rhythm and sway,
this striking mixed couple, while people watch,
sipping drinks on a brown couch,
wondering where she's from, and how he pulled her.

And then my glimpse is gone,
and I'm driving again through the rain,
but there it is, in my stomach, a knowing;
I was born of a love pitted against the norm,

born of bold and different dreams.

WHY I HATED YOU AT THE BUS SHELTER

The green wellies are offensive and signal everything I want
to leave behind during my evening out, yet, Dad, you insist

on wearing them, and keep moaning that you've driven 30 miles,
walked two, to drop me off at this bus shelter, where all the other

Llanbedr teens meet, condemned as we are to live in lonely hillside
houses on bible-black streets. I long only to be deep in that shelter,

hiding from the piecing lights of the SPAR, feeling Leon's lips
pressed tight, the hot surge of inexperienced tongue, tasting of hooch

and stolen fags, so all I ask is that you don't get out the car, Dad,
in those wellies, because it's hard enough being mixed, with massive

bushy hair and living deep in the sticks with no telly, without you
dropping me off in our crappy rusty Bedford van, sheepdog barking

like mad in the back, and you standing there in your wellies, for all
to see – the ultimate *joskin* thing to do. Can't you see I'm living

in the in-between here, Dad, always on the borderlands, always left out?
So can't you let me have this surprise bus shelter invite to hang out

with the popular kids? But you do get out and stand there, rooted,
wanting a hug – *You're ashamed of me, Emily? Just get back in the van*

and please leave now, Dad, I hiss, and your eyes fill. As you turn away,
your tufty head catches the glow of the streetlamp, a little bent over

in your battered khaki wax jacket, trailing a smell of mud and imperial
leather soap. You climb into the driver's seat, engine roars, exhaust fumes,

dog barking getting fainter, now only the loud voices of the boys
trying to penetrate Welsh village silence. I stand apart, flooded

by this image of you, while all other longings drift like the smoke
from their Benson and Hedges into the sharp winter's night.

NO POINT CRYING OVER SPILT MILK

16th birthday high tea is telegraph-wire taut.
Dad talking too loudly. Trying desperately to peg
a nice conversation on a pre-break-up memory.
Mum corpse-still in a stiff chair. Charm-immune.

Dad travelling through the busy café to order,
his gait jolly. Back with tray piled high –
thick yellow slabs of clotted cream, wobbling fat dollops
of raspberry jam in silver dishes, yellow scones, milk in a little jug,
tea in a proper fancy Portmeirion tea pot.

He's beaming, shouting, *I've got 'the works'*
approaching unsteadily. A lurch, a fall. Tray crashes.
Mosaic of broken plates, jam in cream, tea raining down
on a posh lady's coat. Dad's best bottle-green cord trousers
and Guernsey jumper are red and white.

Whole café watching. Dad's *So sorry so sorry so sorry* –
ineptly gathering things up.
Look on Mum's face – unpitying wall.
Yet another disappointment.
Dad on his knees mopping up cream with blue roll.
The scones are still salvageable,
there's no point crying over spilt milk.

Realising I have never loved him harder.

I LIVE HERE

An old lady, all permed grey hair and glasses,
her gun cocked and loaded,
words honed to pierce Mum's skin
as she shops in the village SPAR,
she fires from narrow pink lips:
When are you going back to Africa?
Mum pauses. She was choosing
a yogurt from the fridge
in her red beret and muddy wellies,
and in polished Welsh, replies;
Rwy'n byw yma. I live here.
Mum puts the yogurt in her basket
and walks down the aisle. Slowly. Regally.
Bullet, missed.

MAMI'S VISIT

That winter, Mum went quiet,
as if December froze her warm tongue
silent as the morning snow,
and everything was strange.
But as the flurries piled, you arrived
smelling of cloves and lavender oil,
our Mami from Martinique.

The *Cwm* was sheep, damp and mud in the morning.
You were fresh cinnamon rolls, at night-time,
tisane laced with dark rum,
ricola herbal sweets and Creole stories —
each one seemed to end in a drowning.

You warmed our school clothes on the Aga,
massaged Mum's feet, plaited cornrows,
clomped out in Dad's wellies to feed the horses —
neat *chignon* in a woolly hat versus barrelling Welsh wind.

Dad said you burnt too much wood,
consumed dwindling reserves with 'astonishing rapidity'.
You poked at the grate, threw another log on the fire,
fierce in your war against the crippling cold.

When January froze water pipes,
you filled kettles for her bath of herbs,
baked uneconomical *gateau economique* —
eight eggs, half a kilo of sugar — a delicious extravagance.
Il faut manger, you told her, and so she did.

You left with the first delicate tendrils of Spring.
At the station, we ate cake wrapped in serviettes,
warm sunlight pooling on the quiet platform,
Mum's Afro shining in a yellow headband,
her tongue alive with words and crumbs.

J'ÉTAIS BELLE

J'étais belle, Mami tells me, *I was beautiful*,
unplaiting her long black hair on her billowing pink bed,
78 and no sign of grey. Long strands pool
over the yielding slope of chestnut shoulders,
embroidered white nightgown ruffled over strong legs.
Rough hands work quickly, hands never permitted to rest,
but each finger elegant, agile, skin under each nail a new-born pink.
She smiles, dark eyes shining with memory.
Tu es belle, Mami. Maintenant.

ON STAYING CLOSE

We didn't notice how, slowly,
every day after the stroke
your body grew tired.

One day, your hand is so shaky
your writing bounces off the lines
on ruled paper, and every one
of your birthday cards
has to be read twice
just to make sure we catch
your escaping words.

Then, you struggle
to screw on a bottle top,
flailing hands refusing to encircle,
fingers dancing theatrically
as if conducting a symphony –
not putting a lid on the coke.

On another day, you return to your boat
and falter on the narrow gangplank,
wobbling, holding yourself steady with a rope.

I ask if you want to take my hand.
Don't treat me like a child, you say,
but don't go – stay close.

BIRTHDAY CARD

Your scrawl after the stroke is light across the page,
fragile as a moth's wing, your veined hand

still bending to your will despite doctor's warnings.
Your stories, Dad, I know have been

a rarely noticed soundtrack to my life. Now,
I picture you bending over your grate, balling newspaper

tightly, as you always did, and telling me another tale
from your kaleidoscopic life. I know that next time

I shall listen, with intent, commit all to memory
just as now I rest on each faint word

webbed across my birthday card
wishing me another healthy, happy year.

DISAPPEARING DAD

Dad, you wave me goodbye
as you always do, both arms swaying wide,
and I remember my embarrassment –
you at the station, me leaving for uni.
Alongside my moving train you ran,
stopping only at the platform end,
then becoming distant and smaller
still waving, still smiling.
Everybody looking.

Now, for me, the old familiar feeling,
my tiny, disappearing Dad,
older now, but still all heart,
still waving, still smiling,
while, blinking back the sting,
I pull away.

FÜR ELISE

Upright in the metal bed,
pink scarf wrapped around
your balding head like a sunset,
the morphine haze lets your phone slip
in its leather granny case, pink to match,
through your cramped fingers.

We ring and search; you can't
remember when you had it last;
repetitions of *I'm sorry* drive us mad
with pity. Perhaps, when they moved
your disappearing body to change the sheets,
it was bundled up in nurse efficiency.

In the basement, we search through
piles of sheets from the palliative ward
trapped in high metal cages.
Finally, it rings its pretty tune,
Für Elise's longing notes filling
the heart of the hospital machine.

Written for an unrequited love,
Beethoven's masterpiece was found
forty years after his death.
Forty years ago, it was the tune
you were playing, piano ringing
through our Welsh farmhouse,
while I watched dust mites'
sunbeam dance, hoping you'd finish
and play again in an endless loop of music.

Later, they give your phone and its pink leather case
to my sister-in-law.
I ask her if she'll keep the ring tone.
Für Elise. For another forty years of love.

THINGS WE MIGHT HAVE DONE ON YOUR BIRTHDAY

On this day, on your birthday, we might have gone to the spa.

You would steam your Caribbean bones in the hottest room and chat (a little too loudly) and laugh (for a little too long) about the films you were watching, the books you were reading and all the things that were getting you through this ungodly dark winter month of January.

You'd refuse to go in the plunge pool and watch me dive into the freezing waters as if I were mad, but I'd know you were proud of this wild girl you'd birthed.

Or we might have a high tea in a country hotel, feeling mischievous and out of place in our too-bright clothes, you, smiling, coconut-oiled, brown and beautiful in a jazzy post-box red coat, me with my big curly Afro, and we would try and pretend to be posh. You would charm the waiter so much he would think that it really had been a long time since he met such an elegant, warm and remarkable lady. He would stop and talk to you for longer than he should, while the other tables look on feeling miffed that this elderly beauty was causing their bellies to rumble.

Or we might just go for a walk, and you wouldn't have quite the right shoes and, in a role-reversal, I'd be exasperated and take your arm so you didn't slip in the frost. We would go to the local park, and you'd pronounce the name of the park wrong, in the French accent that you clung onto so stubbornly for fifty years in this country, and it would sound so glamorous. And with you on my arm, and your delight in the way the light shone through the trees, the way the frost sparkled in the sunshine, and *how those red berries crown that holly*, it wouldn't feel like the local Leeds park at all but strolling arm-in-arm through *Les Champs-Élysées*, or Kew gardens or some entirely more exciting place altogether.

And you'd say, as you always did, that you loved me and were so proud of me because you knew that there wasn't such a thing as telling somebody you loved them *too* many times and I would feel the most special girl in the world, even though I was a middle-aged woman, and then we'd laugh at something daft and know that we were the only two people in the world that would find that funny.

But instead, I clear the frosted leaves from your grave, feeling guilty that it doesn't look as smart as your neighbour's. I've forgotten to bring flowers, again, so I try and put together a bouquet with holly and fir. *It's still not done*, I hear you say, you who were so good at making a bunch of straggly flowers look splendid, so I add a branch of yellow leaves and the colour really pops. I stand back to admire my handywork, knowing that when I get home, I'll play your favourite Bill Withers song loudly and dance in the kitchen with my kids and that will be the real place for celebration, not here. Happy earth-day Mum. *It's going to be a lovely day*.

SMALLER THINGS

We were like fields once, you and I,
friends side by side under azure skies
joined by a protecting wall
observing everything.

No two days the same: watching
fat waterboatmen diving
towards the river's bed;
spotting unexpected swirls
in the milky way after
a summer's day; inhaling
fir trees after rain.

Now I deal in dereliction
and cold winds drift me rootless,
so, I look for smaller things,
keep them in my sight:
a mottled tadpole's growing legs,
the curl of an unfurling fern,
a river's ever-shattered light.

THE AUGUST WIND BLOWS THROUGH THE SYCAMORES

and spins the green leaves silver.
All promise of Spring long gone,
the woods are tired.

Crows pick at sour, come-too-early blackberries
as whispers of autumn
rise from the forest floor.

Towering cow parsleys are storm-bent;
wild raspberries have lost their early tang;
froths of meadowsweet are browning at their tips;

and us, what of us?

We will walk on towards summer's end,
knowing all that we have lost
can grow again.

RETREAT
For Kayta

At the retreat, we are to rise early to connect with our chakras.
The ladies are ready; serene, poised, legs crossed, bare feet
in prayer position.

Piled high with dry wood, the fireplace sparks into the whitewashed
room while crystals curve the sun's rays into rainbows
on windowsills.

On rusting hooks, dreamcatchers web our dreams.
The ladies' faces are sky-open, ready for transportation,
for journeying.

So, when the feather-soft teacher's voice asks us to close our eyes
and breathe deep into each chakra,
they are set for lift off.

I lie on the mat, inhale, try to let stillness deep into lungs,
to let it move outwards, to heart, groin, head, limbs;
yet there is only bubbling twitchiness,

the familiar, constant Spring-like energy urging arms
to move, legs to run, eyes to open.
I am sitting on an ant's nest.

Beyond the crystals I see the fell, imagine only running fast
up its rough-hewn, rain-soaked slopes, chakras in wild spin.
But then I start to imagine

this inability to lie quiet – this spring, as a grain of rough sand. Like
an oyster, I will cover it with protective layers.
Incurable – my defect and my treasure.

Over time, let it become pearled in my body's shell.

III: OTHER WILD

LEFT

There are three of them; tiny, coiled commas,
tender snouts tucked into soft pink bellies,
spikes still yielding. Alone in long allotment grass
on a heat-blurred summer's day,

not moving to the touch, my children scoop
them into jumpers, carry them careful as eggs,
house them in a paper-lined box, watch their petal
tongues lap cool water and name them.

When I ask why they were alone, the RSPCA lady explains:
For 6 to 8 weeks, hoglets are fed by their mothers.
Disturb a nest and she can abandon (or eat) her babies.
Sometimes, mother will leave for no discernible reason.

I think of lost, dehydrating hoglets in the sun,
and an abandoning mother. Does she feel an ache of
loss that stills her in her busy hunt for worms?
Or does she live freely in new self-filled days,
without the bonds of nests, of babies?

THE PTARMIGAN

In the Cairngorm peaks,
the ptarmigan, rare bird,
is ling-heather-blending
brown in summer,
bobbing barely visible,
errant tuft of tundra,
on the vast plateau.

But in winter, she's white,
her soft feathers turning
the colour of long-enduring snow
in the tug of seasons.

This lies now in patches
under the baking sun,
edges devoured, retreating,
pouring into clear-flowing brooks and burns.

The summits now stand naked,
unblanketed all season.
Granite shimmers in the light.
And the ptarmigan – does it now forget
its feathers once turned white?

TALL TALE

Frost glitters in the lamplight on their walk home from the pub.
Why did you tell them God made me from your rib, Adam? she asks.
That's a pretty improbable story, even for you.
How many pints have you had? Where's your missing rib then?

He can feel the heat of her anger even though he can't see
her face properly. He doesn't know what to say.
He can't admit, *Eve, people love your stories.*
I can't capture their attention. I wanted to shine for a moment.

He stays quiet.

Eve continues: *And then there's all that stuff you said about the snake*
and the apple. We both agreed to leave Eden because it was boring –
and I don't even like apples.

Adam reaches out to take her hand as they shut
the garden gate behind them.
I promise I'll set the record straight tomorrow, he says, pulling her in close.
I don't think they were really listening, anyway.

BREEZE

Darkness burns, and truths
maim and bruise,
burrow deep into heart-space.

I cling to you, my life ring,
feel the slick of your night-time sweat
on lips and fingertips.

The humidity stifles –
no break in the clouds.
Under a ceiling of grey,

we thrash and bleed.
Love slices and makes the crying last,
pushes friends to leave and floors you.

You walk across our narrow room,
torso moonish in the half-light.
You open the window and the breeze cools,

blows scents of summer grass
fragrant with tomorrow
clean across tear and cum-stained sheets.

ELSEWHERE

You bring me a sprig of honeysuckle on my breakfast tray.
Elsewhere, war is breaking out, people leave belongings and chickens;

the elderly lady must walk the dusty road to somewhere safer;
while, on Ward 57, the little girl is discharged for a few days

while her parents smile that tight smile;
elsewhere, a boy falls into the canal on his bike, everybody

rushes to help, and he emerges muddied, laughing; elsewhere,
a couple look for somewhere to make love on the riverbank –

there was something about watching his wife swim in the river
that morning, the way the light caught her hair, waist and thighs;

elsewhere, two people who should have left each other long ago
turn their backs to sleep on opposite sides of the bed, knowing

they are only half living. You bring me honeysuckle
on a breakfast tray, and who knows what made you pluck it

this very morning, but the scent of it,
the shape of it, the gift of it keeps me here.

HIDE AND SEEK

I

The counting's long over
yet still I hide
waiting for capture
in a game abandoned
by all but me
who still
wants to be found.

II

Lately, I have been remembering
the taste of the coffee on your tongue
as the sunlight corners the outside wall,
your long body striped by slatted blinds,
my morning tiger sleeping gentle
before the roar of daytime

NURSE CHARLOTTE

After Roger Robinson

Into our carnival of despair comes
Nurse Charlotte with her smell of Nivea

and wide brown eyes. She is the one
who rushed our girl up to Intensive Care,

who seemed to know just what to say and do,
and so young too, travelling with us and the hospital bed

in the lift, her gentle talk on the threshold
between urgency and warmth. I notice her socks

are adorned with little bows as she leads us
to two chairs before our knees give way.

The resuscitation room is orange and our girl
is a floppy doll, smooth-headed under

the hospital sheet. Nurse Charlotte sits upright
and so neatly, with her feet side-by-side

on the freshly bleached vinyl floor. *She will
pull through*, she tells us, and her long,

mascaraed lashes flutter like a wren's wing,
like a beating heart and I know it's going

to be okay because I have accepted
Nurse Charlotte's gift of conviction,

seeded it deep in my being, and there
it grows, rooted as steady as her

two Clarks' brogues planted
so firmly on the ground.

CARTWHEELING

On our last shopping trip,
at your insistence we bought
sports bras and crop tops
but this evening you pulled
your t-shirt off,
thin torso throwing long shadows
across the summer grass.

You cartwheel,
then look at me with narrowed eyes;
I know I was too loud
at school pick-up, my laughter
honked all over the playground.

I stretch my legs out on the picnic blanket,
pick a daisy and push it into my hair,
watch your lithe body somersault
then fall back into a crab.
The flower is embarrassing.

In this evening light I see,
crowning your forehead,
a fuzz of fine baby hairs,
and there, below your nipple,
the operation scar.

Last night, still happy
to watch *The Little Mermaid,*
you tell me
The mermaid had no tears;
it's why she suffers more.

Dandelion puffs swim through the air,
on one of them, my prayer.

Cry all your tears loudly, Rose,
and, top off, honk with laughter.
Feel the summer breeze on bare skin.
Forget princes; cartwheel
and try wearing daisies in your hair.

OLUWALE RISING

We are gathered in the council chambers, and I watch this white, middle-aged man-manager, who has always been listened to, raise his voice in his own defence to explain that Black Lives Matter is the wrong kind of Black anger and David Oluwale's life is *too* tragic.

After all, he wants some hope in the messaging for his company to get behind, and as for our plans to commemorate David – well, thinking of certain statues recently, they have become a dangerous rallying ground for angry people, haven't they? A site of Black rioting. And besides, to stand by us and our campaign is like picking sides in a football team, isn't it, so he can't be seen to be supporting Chelsea over Man City, can he...?

What I mean, he says, because our company is not political, we must remain neutral and that means no to your sculpture in commemoration of a man hounded to his death in the Aire by policemen, and yes, I am unravelling promises made, but you must understand my position. My hands are tied.

I watch his red face and I stare at the walls and then I see it. It's not just Black anger around this pillared room with high ceilings and teak tables, its white and Brown, it's historic, it's from before and now and later. It's *I can't breathe*. White silence equals violence, no justice, no peace. Is my son next?

It's storming and flooding the room with Middle Passage sea water as heavy as a leg-iron, and it's bursting with the feeling in Oluwale's gut when he struck back against that policeman beating him with baton and got his head beaten in; it's strong with his stubbornness of sleeping in the same doorway, returning to it night after night knowing that the officers would find him there. It smells of policemen's piss, it smoulders with the fire they lit on his newspaper bedding; it's as dark as the Middleton woods at midnight where they threw him out of the van patchworked with bruises to see if he would be able to find his own way back to his stinking doorway.

All of this is building in the centre of the room, and even if it's only unleashed in moderate tones now, it will grow and spread and this manager man will pay for his cowardice. A riot is the language of the unheard. It begins here.

WITCH

Roll the word around your mouth
and let it conjure, do its work,

spell-bind, because it's calling you.
Think! Does it sound like fear

and midnight curses or feel like power,
pulsing with deep-time knowing?

They say a coven is 12 –
13 with the devil – but he never helped

the thousands of outcast sisters,
annihilated by men in fire and water.

We women of appetite enjoy the pull
of trembling flesh, of hot breath,

of our naked natural selves.
We book readers, thinkers,

nonconformers, wise ones, radicals,
we are the crones, the whores, the spinsters

of healing and herbs, the women with
secrets, the ancestral whisperers.

We are Obeah women with Asante
understandings, Cailleach hags

of Scotland, the ghosts of Pendle and Salem.
We are *all* witches – it's just a matter

of how many parts of our witchery
we decide to hide.

I'LL SHOW YOU MINE AND YOU SHOW ME YOURS

For a box of milk tray
For a pound
For a packet of salt and vinegar crisps
For a kiss

Amy showed him hers, in the rhododendron bushes
in the school yard – because he was the head boy.

She went quiet all week and her cheeks flushed pink
with the crawling memory of it, while he watched her closely
across the classroom, sharpening his pencils
and enjoying the new feeling that
surged up like Spring sap through his veins.

And so, after Amy, he cornered Samantha, but she
was harder to convince and wacked it with her lunch box.

Jennifer in Year 5 was easier to persuade, but cried
while she lowered her knickers and tried to focus
on all the strawberry laces
she could buy for a pound in the tuck shop,

but that pound never came, nor the milk tray,
nor the salt and vinegar crisps, and nobody wanted
a disgusting kiss from him.

So, the girls brought in gifts for each other and decided to carry
their hard plastic lunch boxes all breaktime, ready to smash it,
should they need to.

LANE SHARE

His red speedos embrace thick, muscular thighs,
his dive a perfect arch; barely a ripple reaches me.
He swims up my lane, a quick precise crawl,
tanned arms breaking the cobalt blue.

He has decided on his direction of travel;
goggles glinting, his stroke tells me
he is not a man who likes to share lanes,
and I am an irritating interloper, a mishap,
a hitch in his showstopping swim.

I swim straight for him (I was here first),
and he relents just before impact,
moves over, muscled jaw twitching
as I glide by, the winner of our watery duel.

DICK PIC

Sent by an important poet,
an erection in shorts
sitting in her WhatsApp
like a stone.

The interview had gone well;
she, a fellow poet
but to him only
a dick pic recipient.

His clothes look dirty;
a two-fingered zoom
proves a patch of mould
blossoming on the cotton
at the base of his crotch.

An old canary now, but still he
sings his song of greatness,
assured that his body
and attention are a gift.

Who told him he could still
slay hearts at seventy?
Who fed him such spoonfuls of flattery
that his ego grew this fat with it?

Strange that what disturbs her most
are the unwashed shorts.
She keeps zooming in –
that patch of mould, spreading
its spores, blooming.

TO THE RANGE ROVER ASSHOLE

March wind grazing my face like sandpaper,
fingers iced to my handlebars,
Range Rover man beeps loudly, then overtakes,

cuts in, pushes me out of the right-turn lane.
Swerving to miss him, I feel the swell
of furious, frightened tears.

I'm a woman on a bike.
You're a man in a massive Range Rover,
do not try and fucking intimidate me!

I'm shouting now. It's self-defence, survival.
It's for all the women pushed out of their lanes
by Range Rover men.

At the lights, he winds his window down,
an amused sneer:
Haha, it's my choice, love, get a car.

My retort, lost in a roar of exhaust fumes:
Never my choice, *love,* to share lanes
with Range Rover assholes like you.

CONDUIT

It's Christmas Eve and I dream I have a third baby.
I give birth in secret, very much alone
in an old Victorian hospital, with one quiet doctor.
She is premature, and I have forgotten everything
I know about raising babies.

I keep forgetting to pick her up and feed her.
I read books for too long or go for lengthy walks instead.
Slowly, she becomes translucent – in the moonlight I can see
all her tiny veins. I ask the doctor if this is right
as I watch her breathe, a coiled and tiny comma in her metal cot.

He says I have to work it out for myself,
and I suddenly remember that she should have breast milk
and maybe biscuits, but looking at her closely, I realise
that she isn't my baby at all, but a wild creature
who can fend for herself.

She smiles and her eyes glitter and shine. I say goodbye,
setting off on foot to bathe in the night-time river.
With each stride I am lifted closer to the stars.

TO SMELL LIKE SKY

Wind, hear me,
I have a gift for you;
it smells like love
but do you want it?

Wind, take me,
for I am sliced,
folded, divided;
my dreams descend
and cannot land.

Wind, scatter me,
for love weighs heavy.
Lift it from me
and bestow a gift
that smells like sky.
Hollow me
so I may fly.

MARDI GRAS UNDER THE FREEWAY[2]

As Miss Delphine steps out the door,
she pauses. The sunlight skids up from the sidewalk,
rests on her bright orange, handstitched Ankara dress,
scatters across the wooden slats to hit
her beaded shoes, creating constellations.

On the steps of her porch,
she feels the drum-roll tremble, the street-shake
of processions drowning out the traffic-drone.

The spirit grips her, arches her back
like that morning sunbeam cornering the doorframe,
kicks her feet above her knees. Now she's spinning
across hurricane-split paving, is dancing the dance
of Black skin worn thin, now rising and shining
in the blare of brass and thumping drums.

She walks towards the dark of the underpass
under the segregating highway; a trombone wail
turns her liquid. She hip-rolls her seventy-year-old body,
tricking time as it follows the pitching rhythm of the band.

From this corner of the city, she joins the rising call
for freedom from under the freeway
with a fierceness so bright that
when Miss Delphine walks home that night
she knows the stars cannot shine
brighter than her people or
the shimmer of her dancing shoes.

---

2 In New Orleans' Tremé, a predominately Black neighbourhood, the
1968 elevated extension of the Interstate 10 freeway erased a vibrant
business corridor and devasted the community. They name it 'the monster'
and it is held up as a prime example of how transportation projects have
exacerbated historic racial inequities in cities across the US.

I NEED MILK TOO

for Kamau Brathwaite and Joseph Zobel

So you tell us, once again, from hospice bed,
91-years-old, baby-blue pyjamas, black scalp glistening,
about the little boy who stole your milk.

He forced your mother's brown nipple
into his wet mouth
my milk   you tell us   taken deep   into his gullet.
Oh you needed love too, love too.

He stole your nourishment,
suckled hard, the white baby, head nestled
behind the curve of her brown breast.
You were alone, comfortless.
Oh you needed love, love too.

How to understand
all of this   this lack   this fury?
You cannot stitch together memories of her
you have lost   thread   you have lost   needle
your pain, those pains, that burning.
You needed love too   you needed milk, too.

When you wake, you cannot always remember the dream –
her calloused palms, your mother, holding the spread of morning sky,
the white sheet she wrapped you in, tightly.

Olive oil glistens on her skin, red cotton dress
billowing in an early harmattan. This is all you have. One more loss
in a chain of lack reaching far from Ghana.

You need love too. You needed milk too.

He stole your milk as she wetnursed his white puckered flesh
as you lay in the green, wind-lashed cane fields
that swallowed your grandmother's body.

At the break of dawn   you rose   and refused to cut the cane.
But he stole your milk and   you are thirsty still.
You need love too.

MARTINIQUE, I HEAR

lullabies in your name, notes singing between syllables;
island of flowers, mother's birthplace, you roll across my
tongue sweet as the swaying of my grandmother's hips

dancing *la beguine.* But under the sweetness, I hear the slash
of cane-cutting cutlasses wielded by ancestors buried
in unmarked graves in your rich red earth. There

I stand, *mulâtresse*, edges of my skirt lifted by warm breezes,
next to the bronze of my grandfather, honouring his world of words,
looking across your southern undulations at the plantation

of his childhood, site of rupture and blood, cutting a trail back
to Benin. Around me hummingbirds seek nectar from deep within
the throats of heliconias, and pelicans dive for silver fish

on the distant rolls of the ocean, and I wonder how your abundance,
a loveliness which nearly hurts the eye, has seen us in chains, how
you've spread the roots of *oiseau-du-paradis* over our rusted manacles.

Are you beautiful, Martinique, to distract us from the blood
dripping down the pages of our past? Martinique, I hear lullabies
in your name, but I must not sleep.

BLODEUWEDD[3]

Waiting above the wooded valley for March winds
to throw ripples in arcs across the glassy llyn,
I burn, standing still on Cwm Croesor's slopes of slate,
feeling the drumbeat of my heart,
the boiling of my blood, the need beneath my belly,
the longing in my yet unopened eyes.

Conjured by magicians from frothy heads of meadowsweet,
woven in silk leaves of oak, spears of August broom,
imprisoned in my form crafted for the needs of men
who crave to stroke my yet unparted thighs,
I'm stifled in my floral stink.

But for the love of Gronw Pebr, I plot my husband's
death at dusk – to be pierced by Gronw's spear.
He shifts his shape from bird to man, survives the forceful blow.
I flee the men on foot, but Gwydion casts a spell
and I become a hated owl, my life supposed a hell.

Now owl, talons sharpened, I've waited until winter
when snow engulfs Yr Wyddfa, to feel the swell of love
and kill the one who bound me. I'm free to fly the valley
and live away from men, quickly shedding every softly scented bud.
I sweep along the cwm on glowing moonlit wings
guided only by the yearnings of my blood.

---

3. Blodeuwedd or Blodeuedd, meaning 'flower-faced', is a central figure in the
Welsh legends of the *Mabinogion,* the 12/13th century collection of folk tales in
Middle Welsh. She was the wife of Lleu Llaw Gyffes in Welsh mythology, and
she was created by a spell from the flowers of broom, meadowsweet and oak
by the magicians Math and Gwydion. She fell in love with Gronw Pebr and was
punished for her adultery, and for plotting to kill her husband, by being turned
into an owl, the 'most hated of birds'.

WHAT TO CALL ME?

Many different women
jostle for room:

the Lost One grapples in shadows while
Professor Confident remains unphased,
fighting krakens in the icy Wharfe
before morning porridge.

Ms Nostalgia sleeps deep under
the heavy duvet of the past,
homesick for places
she is yet to visit.

Dr Hope, born many times
but still unformed,
speaks in hushed tongues.

We listen out for her;
she knows our names
and where to take us.

WOMEN ARE ONLY FREE,

my daughter tells me, during those
few steps when she walks
from her father's arm
to her husband's embrace.

We contemplate this.

Perhaps, we decide, she should,
in those sweet in-between seconds,
strip off her dress and veil,
run naked down the aisle,
rejoice in the barebones of her being,
scream primal screams up into the eaves
until guests put hands over their ears
and pray for the handover

to be complete, as she, unchained,
becomes wild with the honeyed taste
of freedom on her tongue,
the fleeting joy of unbelonging
coursing through her veins.

YOU TELL ME A DESIRE LINE
For Ellis

You tell me a desire line
is the name for the quickest way
to get somewhere,
ignoring all official paths
cutting new trails, guided only by
the route need takes you.

Now I see them everywhere –
furrowed tracks slicing corners,
snaking towards hidden views,
long grass pressed flat as lovers seek
quiet spaces or parents take kids
to spots to pee under canopies of trees.

Let disobedient feet cross fresh earth,
work ways down small illicit paths,
cut through boundaries and unspool
desire lines across the summer grass.

WHEN I EMPTIED MY MOON-CUP ON THE MOUNTAIN

I emptied my moon cup
on the flanks of the great mountain,
and watched my blood sink into starry mosses.
Then the mountain spoke:

I used to attract monks on holy pilgrimages,
journeying priests – then nothing.
So, I have slept a thousand years,
roused only now by blood libation.

Let me help, I replied,
to return you to your former glory.
I seek no glory, the mountain said,
But if it pleases, worship me thus:

When you climb my flanks, gather
juicy cloudberries, sharp fresh mint.
Inhale them deep and you'll carry me with you
but will leave with less weight than you bring.

Sleep on me; they say you will wake
mad or a poet. Choose both
and the right words will follow you sure as swifts.
I can raise you closer to the sun,

but don't just reach for the heavens.
Listen to my rumblings, the songs of clear streams,
caves and crevasses – these are my heartbeats;
it is through the ears I share my wildscapes.

And if you climb me once again
when your body feels the monthly pull
of blood and moon and tide,
please, awake me with libation.

LET ME MAP YOU, HE SAID

I'll trace your contours with my pen,
draw your ridges, hidden coves,
commit to paper the features
of your hills and valleys.

But you will only find my outline,
your charts will not determine
the storms that carve my bays,
the stillness of my caves.

I shall write you then, he said,
in sonnets and in prose,
distil in verse wrinkles between brows
and harmony of leg and arm and waist.

You'll miss the beating of my temple,
the smell I leave behind on my side of the bed,
the shape the battered backs of my old slippers take,
the sharpness of my early morning breath.

And only in the days before I bleed
will your fingers burn
from the anger swelling in my belly.
My salty fissures and my cracks

in words cannot be tracked;
they live unchartered, uncontained
beyond a world of facts.
So, this body will remain
unmapped.

ACKNOWLEDGEMENTS

Rose and Theo, I watch you grow and try and capture some of the miracle of your presence in my life on the page. Tom Brown, you anchor my boat with your love and have done for 28 years. Thank you. Peter Marshall, you'll be pleased to see more poems about you in this collection! Your unending love of life is intoxicating – thank you for passing the thirst for experience down to me. Liz Ashton-Hill, you are always the most thoughtful and careful critic of my work, I'm grateful. Dylan, little brother, thank you for your warmth and depth of thought. Charlotte Zobel, beloved cousin, you keep me smiling. I am blessed.

For long discussions whilst hiking in wildscapes I thank Vanja Celebicic, Lee Snoding and Bridget Walker. We know that the unexamined life is not worth living and share an awe of the natural world. Ruth Thomas, Rose Farrar, Ellis Burgin, Richard Lester, Bridget and Vanja, your friendship lifts and sustains me.

Jeremy Poynting thank you for your diligence and calm, clear guidance in the creation, editing and delivery of this book and to Hannah Bannister for facilitating the whole process so expertly. Kezia Lewis, your beautiful cover art has brought *Other Wild* to life, my gratitude for your talent. Thanks again to Khadijah Ibrahiim, Malika Booker, Melanie Abrahams, Jacob Ross, Sai Murray and Jason Allen-Paisant for helping to keep the poetry scene thriving in in Leeds. Sai, it's always a joy to share poems with you, thank you for your thoughts and company. As ever, I am grateful to my dear friends and colleagues at Leeds Beckett University: James McGrath, Caroline Herbert, Rob Burroughs, Rachel Rich and Susan Watkins. You have supported me in essential and myriad ways over the years. Dyfrig Jones, you keep me connected to my Welsh roots and the landscapes of Eryri. Diolch am dy gyfeillgarwch.

Poetry groups keep our community afloat – my thanks to everyone in John Whale's poetry group for your careful feedback on my developing work, to the Peepal Tree Press Readers and Writers group for being a constant source of support and scrutiny, and to Marva McClean for creating the 'Strong in the Broken

Places' online poetry community – a labour of love. Katie Brown, Hannah Sherbersky, Max Farrar, Cathy Thomas, Liz, Ed, James, Lewis and Molly Brown and Sue Bone – you are family and the foundation from which I grow. Jenny Zobel – Mum – your absent presence fills every page of this book. I live in gratitude for your unconditional love.

Thanks to *Dreamcatcher* for publishing earlier versions of these poems:

"Try to Map Me, She Said", *Dreamcatcher*, Issue 44, 2022
"How You Rose", *Dreamcatcher*, Issue 47, 2023
"Why I Hated You at the Bus Shelter", "Martinique" and "Nurse Charlotte", *Dreamcatcher*, Issue 50, 2024

ABOUT THE AUTHOR

Emily Zobel Marshall is of French-Caribbean and British heritage and grew up in the mountains of Eryri in North Wales. She is a Professor in Postcolonial Literature at Leeds Beckett University. She is an expert on the trickster figure in the folklore, oral cultures and literature of the African Diaspora and has published widely in these fields, including her books *Anansi's Journey: A Story of Jamaican Cultural Resistance* (2012, University of the West Indies Press) and *American Trickster: Trauma Tradition and Brer Rabbit* (2019, Rowman and Littlefield).

She plays mas in Leeds West Indian carnival and has established a Caribbean Carnival Cultures research platform and network that aims to bring the critical, creative, academic and artistic aspects of carnival into dialogue with one another. She consults for several arts, historical and educational organisations on decolonial methodologies and approaches and is Co-Chair of the David Oluwale Memorial Association, a charity committed to fighting racism and homelessness. She regularly contributes to discussions on race and racial politics in the media and has interviewed many world-famous writers, artists and musicians, including Chimamanda Ngozi Adiche, LKJ, Gary Younge, Caryl Phillips, Yinka Shonibare and Corinne Bailey Rae.

Emily has had poems published in the Peepal Tree Press anthologies *Weighted Words* and *Sanctuary* (2021, 2024), *Magma*, *Smoke Magazine*, *The Caribbean Writer* and *Stand*. Her poetry collection, *Bath of Herbs*, is described as 'spellbinding' and 'a beautifully crafted, honest and thoughtful first collection which explores the complexity of mixed-race, hybrid identities and relationships to the English and Welsh mountains, fells, rivers and shorelines from an 'othered', unmappable, positionality.'